CUENTO DE LUZ

To all the people who love and care for this colorful world.
—Desrirée Acevedo

The human race is like the perfect picture,
in which all of the different colors combine in perfect harmony.
—Silvia Álvarez

STONE PAPER
NO TREES - NO WATER - NO BLEACH

This book is printed on **Stone Paper©** that is Silver **Cradle to Cradle™** certified.

Cradle to Cradle™ is one of the most demanding ecological certification systems, awarded to products that have been conceived and designed in an ecologically intelligent way.

Certified **B** Corporation

Cuento de Luz™ became a **Certified B Corporation©** in 2015. The prestigious certification is awarded to companies which use the power of business to solve social and environmental problems and meet higher standards of social and environmental performance, transparency, and accountability.

The Color of Your Skin
Text © 2021 Desirée Acevedo
Illustrations © 2021 Silvia Álvarez
© 2021 Cuento de Luz SL
Calle Claveles, 10 | Urb. Monteclaro | Pozuelo de Alarcón | 28223 | Madrid | Spain
www.cuentodeluz.com
Original title in Spanish: *El color de tu piel*
English translation by Jon Brokenbrow
ISBN: 978-84-18302-40-4
1ˢᵗ printing
Printed in PRC by Shanghai Cheng Printing Company March 2021, print number 1834-5

THE COLOR
of Your Skin

Desirée Acevedo & Silvia Álvarez

Vega loved to draw. She imagined that she was a great artist and the refrigerator where her mom hung her artwork was part of a famous museum. Today, she was drawing a special picture for her mom, and hoped it would make it into the gallery when she got home from school!

Her friend Alex stopped by, and peered into the box of pencils Vega had on her table. "Can you lend me the skin-colored pencil, please?" he asked.

"Skin-colored?" said Vega, thoughtfully.

"Do you mean the color of your skin,
or the color of my skin?"

"Or the beautiful brown skin of my neighbor Vincent?
It reminds me of caramel."

"Hang on! Maybe you mean that really light shade of the new girl who just started school. When she blushes, her cheeks look like two bright red apples!"

"Or maybe my mom's. Or my dad's . . ."

"And our music teacher's skin is so pretty . . . maybe you want that color!"

"Or the lady who sells flowers from that little shop in the street. She's always hot, and she gets really red!"

"Um, no, Vega," said Alex, "I mean skin color."

"Skin color?" said Vega.

"Yeah, you know," he replied, "the one that's kind of light pink, and a bit strange."

"But . . . but your skin doesn't look like that. Your skin is a bit like the color of toast!

And mine doesn't either. I'm kind of pale."

Vega and Alex stared into the box of colored pencils.
"So why is 'skin color' called 'skin color'?" they wondered.

"Well," said Vega, "it's very simple. I guess the person who discovered it must have had skin that color, and they just forgot to add the rest of the colors. Everyone makes mistakes!"

So Vega and Alex sat down on the floor and gathered up all of the pencils and crayons and paints they thought could be 'skin color', and the two of them drew a beautiful picture together.

Once they had finished, they proudly looked at their picture, and
Alex gave it to Vega so that she could give it to her mom.

Well, this picture never made it to the refrigerator, because her mom put it in a beautiful frame and hung it on the biggest wall in the family room to remind them always that colors are like hugs: the more, the better!